IGOR

I AM EVA!

By Sarah Willson
Based on the Screenplay by Chris McKenna

Ready-to-Read

Simon Spotlight / Nickelodeon
New York   London   Toronto

Simon Spotlight
An imprint of Simon & Schuster Children's Publishing Division
1230 Avenue of the Americas, New York, New York 10020
Manufactured in the United States of America
First Edition
2 4 6 8 10 9 7 5 3 1
ISBN 13: 978-1-4169-6813-9
ISBN 10: 1-4169-6813-X

My name is Eva.

I live in a kingdom called Malaria.

Igor brought me to life with
the help of his friends, Brain
and Scamper.

Igor said, "I am your master.
You are Eva!"
At least, that is what I heard.
"I am Eva!" I repeated.
"No, no," he replied.

"You are not Eva. You are **Evil!**"
But I liked the name Eva better.
So Eva became my name.

I felt happy the day that I met
my kind new friends—so happy
that I crashed through a wall!

I found more new friends.
We had fun playing.

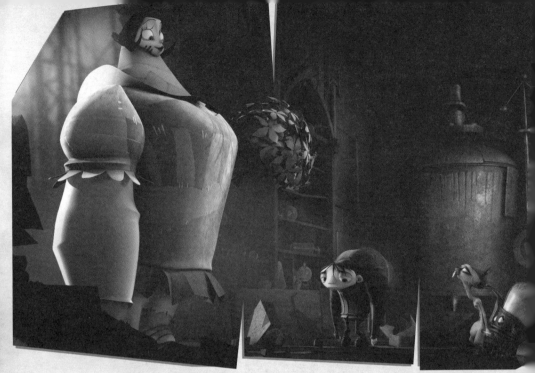

Igor told me, "Stop being so nice!"
But **he** was so **nice** to me!

He gave me flowers.
He made me tea.
He introduced me to his friends.
He even took me
to have my brain washed!

While I had my brain washed,
I watched a show about acting.
That was when I found out that
my dream was to be an actress!

When Igor saw that I wanted to act,
he was upset!
"Who changed the channel?" he demanded.
But I was glad someone did.
Otherwise, how would I have known
I was born for the stage?

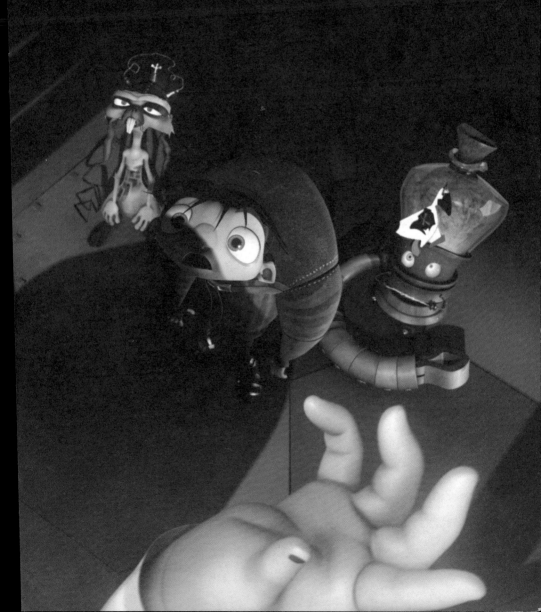

But Igor was still very kind.
He told me I could try out for
a musical!
He said I could sing and dance
during the tryouts.

I would also have to stomp around
and smash stuff onstage.
I thought it was strange.
But I was eager to show everyone
that I was a real actress.

One evening Igor told me that
King Malbert wanted everyone
to do evil things.
"To be someone, you must be evil,"
he said. But I did not think so.
I told Igor I would rather be
a good nobody than an evil
somebody.

I think Igor felt the same way,
but he would not say so.

There was so much to do before
the tryouts.

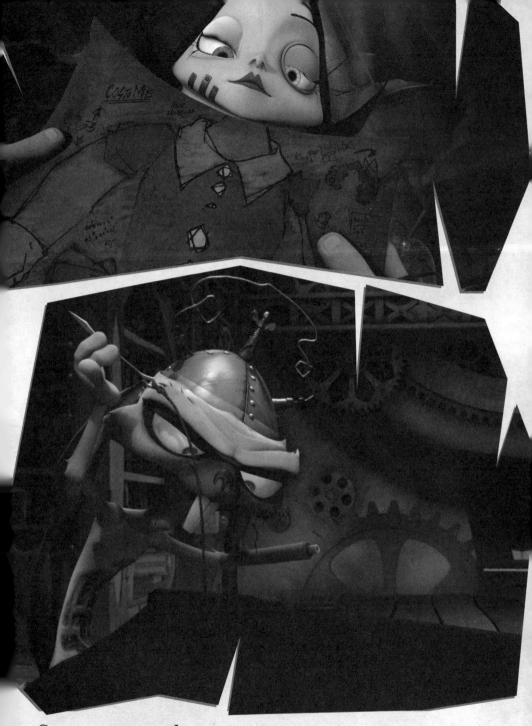

Scamper made my costume.

Brain helped me rehearse my lines.

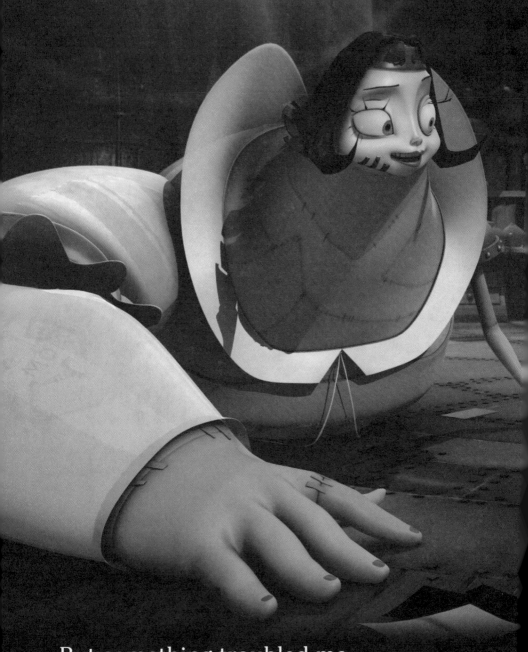

But something troubled me.
Why was it always so dark outside?
Why did everyone think King Malbert
was such a wise ruler?

But I did not stay worried for long.
After all, I had to prepare for
my tryout!

Then things went terribly wrong.
First Igor hurt my feelings.
Soon after, he simply vanished.

A talent agent showed up.
At least, I thought he was
a talent agent.
His name was Dr. Schadenfreude.
He promised to make me a star.

Dr. Schadenfreude tried to make me
do something evil. I refused!
But then he said that Igor was not
my friend, and that Igor liked another
girl better. He even said that I am
a bad actress!
I got so upset, I slapped that man!
Then something inside me changed.
I grew madder and madder.
I felt evil!

It was time for my tryout.

I stomped all over the arena.

I smashed lots of things.

And just when I was ready for
my big finish, I heard Igor's voice.

"You are Eva," Igor said.
"You are good, not evil!
Remember what you told me?
It is better to be a good nobody
than an evil somebody."
Slowly my head began to clear.
He was right. I was **not** evil!
And Igor was my friend, after all.

Suddenly **CRASH!** King Malbert got squashed by his evil machine. The machine had been making the dark clouds and helping the king keep Malaria evil all this time.

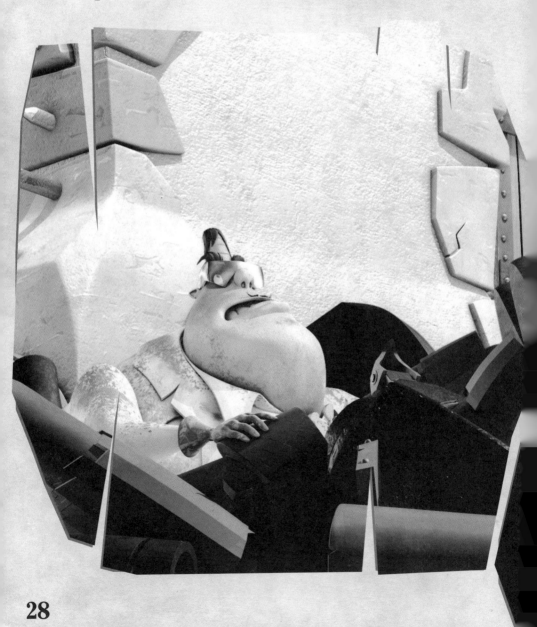

When the machine broke, the sun came out—and everyone cheered!

After that, things really changed.

Malaria was no longer dark.

The scientists stopped being evil.

Dr. Schadenfreude became a pickle-seller.

Igor was elected president!
And as for me?

I am Eva—the actress!